Two Left Feet

Story by Melaina Faranda

Illustrations by Miriam Serafin

Contents

Chapter 1
Another Tumble

Flynn hurtled face-first towards the basketball court. He glimpsed the coach's open-mouthed grimace from the sidelines, even as Flynn flung out his arms to try to break the fall. He winced as his palms scraped against the hard surface of the court just before the rest of his body crashed down heavily to join them.

From where he lay, Flynn could hear the receding *thump*, *thump*, *thump* of the basketball escaping and being swooped upon by the opposing side.

Coach Miguel blew the whistle and sprinted over, with Levi and Josh fast at his heels.

“Are you all right?” Coach Miguel’s forehead creased with concern.

Flynn nodded weakly. He stifled a groan as he shifted into a sitting position to show that he hadn’t broken anything. “I’m okay.” He needed to convince Coach Miguel that he was still good to play. Flynn wanted desperately to be selected for the school’s representative team. The team had risen from being the inter-school underdogs to smashing all the competition for seven seasons in a row! It had become a team so legendary that some parents even enrolled their kids at the school just for the basketball team.

As Levi and Josh helped Flynn to his feet, the coach tried to reassure him. “There’s no real damage, except for those scrapes, but we’ll get something onto those and they’ll heal up in no time.”

Cuts and grazes would eventually fade, Flynn thought, glancing at a dark scab on his knee from a tumble a couple of weeks before. But it would take longer for his pride to heal.

This was Flynn's third fall in the series of lead-up games, which were also informal try-outs for the school team.

Levi and Josh were all-rounders and already a sure thing. Flynn knew he was a good goal shooter, and he could be a fast runner, too. But when he was dribbling the ball, he found it tricky to concentrate on bouncing it while sprinting and dodging his opponent. It was as if he suddenly had two left feet!

Flynn was quiet for the rest of school that day. Coach Miguel hadn't said anything directly, but there would only be a few more games before he made his final decision about who would be included in the team.

If Flynn didn't make it onto the team, he'd miss out on the competition, and also on all the training sessions after school. Joking and mucking about with Levi and Josh were part of the fun. They had all been best friends since Year 1. If Flynn didn't get into the team, he would be alone.

Chapter 2
The Day Gets Worse

The day got worse. Mum had arrived at school to pick up Flynn and his little sister, Amelia, to take her to a new dance school. It meant Flynn would have to sit around at a dance school all afternoon, instead of catching the bus home with Josh. All that morning at breakfast, Amelia had pranced around in a glittery purple dress, flouncing its puffy skirt. She had refused to sit and eat her cereal. Finally, Dad had sighed and muttered, "It's important to start the day with the right fuel. Children who don't eat breakfast might be too weak to dance in the afternoon …"

When they got into the car, Flynn could tell that Mum was stressed from work. And, sure enough, she answered a stream of business calls on the car speaker while they were stuck in a honking traffic jam. Amelia kept herself entertained by singing her favourite song of the moment on repeat.

Flynn had a headache by the time they found a carpark. As usual, they were late.

The dance school was in an old-fashioned brick warehouse. Almost as soon as they had climbed the steps, Mum's phone started to ring again. She glanced at the screen and held up her fingers to signal *two minutes*. Flynn sighed. It was always more than two minutes.

"I think it's still in the car," Mum said to the person on the phone. "No, I'll just go and check." She turned to Flynn and Amelia and mouthed apologetically, *"You two go in. I'll be a little bit longer."*

Amelia skipped through the doorway and Flynn trudged behind.

The woman at the reception desk looked up from a computer and smiled. "Can I help you?"

"Um, my little sister is going to be learning ballet."

She beamed. "Of course. The session has started, so I'll take her through."

Amelia, suddenly shy, clung to Flynn's hand. They wove through a rabbit warren of corridors and doors leading into different rooms, passing empty studios, until they reached Amelia's dance class. The receptionist introduced them briefly and said she had to get back to the desk. Only once Flynn saw how the dance teacher welcomed Amelia to the group did he feel free to return to the reception.

Except Flynn couldn't remember how to get back. It was like being lost in a maze.

Flynn accidentally opened one door onto a kitchen. Then, certain he was meant to turn to the right, he opened another door. A group of kids around his age all stared back at him. They were mostly girls with a few boys scattered amongst them. The teacher held out his arms to gesture Flynn in.

"Here he is! We've been waiting for you. Come in, come in. Class, I'd like you to welcome our newest *danseur*."

Flynn wanted to say that there had been a mistake, that he wasn't a "danseur", that he had two left feet. But the teacher seemed so welcoming and excited to have another student that Flynn felt too embarrassed to show him up. Maybe Flynn could just pretend for a few minutes, then find a quiet moment to let the teacher know that Flynn wasn't who he thought.

"We don't use *Monsieur* and *Mademoiselle* here. You can call me Dai," the teacher said, gesturing to a shelf along one wall. "Find a pair of slippers that fit. Next time, though, you'll need to bring your own."

Chapter 3

A Secret Weapon

"Ballerinas and danseurs, take your place at the barre," Dai instructed.

Flynn self-consciously shuffled in his borrowed black slippers to join the row of other students, who had lined up against a long wooden rail attached to a full-length mirror. He tried to copy the girl in front of him. At first it was a little bit like stretching to warm up for a basketball game, but this felt different – more deliberate.

Flynn waited for a good moment to privately say something to the teacher, but it never came. Instead, the class swept through a series of dance positions as Dai called them out.

Flynn enjoyed the way the movements were slower than basketball. It allowed time for his body to catch up.

Even though he was moving slower than if he'd been at basketball training, the lesson seemed to fly by.

"You have flexibility!" Dai observed approvingly when the class had finished. "And you're a quick learner. I'm glad you chose to come to our dance school. You have the potential to be a good dancer."

This was the moment for Flynn to explain that the teacher must have mistaken him for someone else. Instead, Flynn blurted, "Would ballet make me more coordinated? I mean with other sports and stuff?"

Dai shrugged. "Of course! Many people learn ballet for the pure love of dance, but some people learn because it gives them an edge in their sport. We have world-famous athletes: football players, wrestlers, Olympians – all learning ballet!"

"Could it make me better at basketball?" Fynn asked. "The thing is," he added hurriedly, "I trip over when I'm running and dribbling the ball. It's like I have two left feet."

Dai raised his eyebrows. "Show me your feet."

Flynn wriggled them out of the slippers.

"Your feet look perfectly normal to me. If anything, having those high arches and toes with such an even length make your feet perfect for ballet."

"So, if I learn ballet, I'll get better at basketball?"

Dai laughed. "Ballet will be your weapon."

"My *secret* weapon," Flynn added under his breath.

"But why don't you want to tell anyone?" Amelia pestered Flynn for the hundredth time. They were on their way home from another dance class.

"Just because," Flynn snapped. He had sworn her and Mum and Dad to secrecy. Ballet was going to be his secret weapon.

Also, deep down, he wasn't sure what the other boys' reactions would be if they knew Flynn was learning ballet. Would they tease him for wearing tights? But then again, what about all those people who wore running pants or bike shorts?

Flynn got on well with the other kids in the ballet class. One of the other boys had been dancing since he was four, and Flynn envied his flexibility and grace. But Flynn could also feel how his own body was steadily becoming more balanced. He and Dad had built a barre in the garage and slid an old, mirrored wardrobe door behind it. Each morning Flynn got up early to practise.

It was interesting learning new words, too, and Flynn liked the way Dai pronounced them with a proper French accent. Gliding was *glisser*. Bending was *plier*, *relever* meant to rise. *Etendre* was stretching, *tourner* was turning, *sauter* was jumping and *elancer* meant to dart.

In some ways, they were all things Flynn already had to do on the basketball court – dart and stretch and jump. But as Dai said, good ballet dancers weren't born overnight, they were made through years of practice and hard work. Flynn could feel himself improving, but would it be fast enough for him to be chosen for the basketball team?

Chapter 4

The Coach Makes a Choice

"Over here!" Flynn caught the ball and dribbled it along the court to bounce it towards the hoop. He was getting ready to shoot when his opponent darted across to slap the ball away. Flynn spun around and stumbled. While he flailed to right himself, the other kid snatched the ball and threw it to a teammate. Within minutes, the opposing team scored a goal.

Levi came and clapped Flynn on the back. "It's okay, we're still ahead. Keep going."

Flynn felt miserable, though. This was the final try-out for the representative school team. Coach Miguel had put all the players hoping to be chosen into two teams to play off. Today, he would announce who would be on the team.

Flynn tried to take Levi's advice and plunged back into the game, but he knew that he'd just wrecked his chances for being chosen.

The whistle blew. The game was over. Flynn's team had won by two points. Flynn knew that it could have been three …

"Okay, gather around, everyone," Coach Miguel hollered. "I know you've all been waiting to find out if you're on the rep team. First up, I want to congratulate everyone on their efforts. You've all played well. But as you know, I've had to make the difficult choice of who will be on our inter-school team. We've been undefeated now for seven years running, and this year's team is going to keep up our tradition of winning!"

While the other kids cheered, Flynn stared at the ground. He had blown it back there on the court. Numbly, he heard Coach Miguel announce the names of those selected. Levi and Josh, of course. And a string of other names. That was it then, Flynn hadn't got in. But suddenly, Josh and Levi were by his side. "We're in, we're all in!" Josh shouted.

Levi laughed at Flynn's startled expression. "Your name was called out. We're all on the team."

Coach nodded in Flynn's direction. "There's a bit of work to do, but you're a good goal shooter, Flynn, and you're getting better at dribbling. I'm sure you'll do us proud."

Flynn nodded, blinking back tears. More than ever, he was going to need to practise his secret weapon.

Chapter 5

The Secret Is Revealed ...

Flynn had been put on reserve as a back-up player for most of the season. He didn't complain, because at least he got to train with the others, and he was still part of the team. Still, he suspected that Coach Miguel had doubts about putting him out there on the court too often, in case he had a fall.

It was tough watching the others play while sitting on the bench, secretly hoping someone would get too tired and need to be subbed in for. The team had done well throughout the season, though, and now they were practising for the semi-final next week.

The semi-final was in the morning, and later in the same day, Flynn would be performing in the ballet school's Dance Spectacular.

On the morning of the match, Flynn took his position on the bench along with the other reserves. They were up against a tough team, and soon the scores were tied. Then Levi leapt for the ball at the same time as another of their players, Tom! The two of them smacked into each other and flew sprawling to the court.

Coach Miguel checked that Levi and Tom were okay and, barely glancing at the bench, gestured for two of the reserves to sub in.

Flynn seized his chance. He was up before the other players on the bench knew what was happening. He raced onto the court.

Flynn was filled with a sense of energy and confidence. This was his moment. He dashed along the court, lit up with unstoppable power. He could feel his new flexibility as he expertly stole the ball from an opponent and dribbled it back towards the goal. He took aim, leapt, and dunked it directly through the hoop.

Flynn scored hoop after hoop.

The team won with a landslide victory.

As the other kids crowded around Flynn to congratulate him, Coach Miguel shook his head. “I have to admit, I didn’t see that coming. What’s your secret, Flynn?”

Flynn didn’t have the opportunity to avoid the question. At that same moment, Eliza, one of the girls from his ballet class, came over to congratulate him. Flynn hadn’t seen her in the grandstand.

“Flynn!” Eliza exclaimed. “I didn’t know you played basketball. That’s my brother.” She pointed to the player Flynn had snatched the ball from.

Then Eliza added, “Are you nervous about the Dance Spectacular tonight?” Her question rang out over the congratulatory chatter.

Flynn’s teammates and coach turned to stare.

“Dance Spectacular?” Josh repeated.

Flynn shrugged. “Um, yeah. I’ve been doing ballet.”

“So that’s your secret?” the coach said wonderingly.

Flynn nodded, embarrassed to have been caught out.

Coach Miguel smiled. “Team, I think we’ve just found our edge for the grand final. Flynn, how about you start showing us a few of your moves in our training sessions?”

Flynn shrugged. “Um, okay.”

The coach added, “And who wants to go cheer Flynn on at the Dance Spectacular?”

Flynn tried to hide his smile when Levi and Josh shouted the loudest, “We do!”